This Orchard book
belongs to

_____

_____

_____

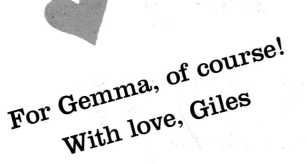
For Gemma, of course!
With love, Giles

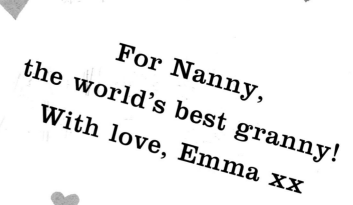
For Nanny,
the world's best granny!
With love, Emma xx

ORCHARD BOOKS

Carmelite House

50 Victoria Embankment

London EC4Y 0DZ

First published in 2015 by Orchard Books

First published in paperback in 2015

ISBN 978 1 40833 590 1

A CIP catalogue record for this book is available from the British Library.

1 3 5 7 9 10 8 6 4 2

Printed in China

Orchard Books

An imprint of Hachette Children's Group

Part of The Watts Publishing Group Limited

An Hachette UK Company

www.hachette.co.uk

MIX
Paper from
responsible sources
FSC
www.fsc.org
FSC® C104740

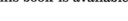

I love my granny

Giles Andreae & Emma Dodd

ORCHARD

I love my granny. Can you tell?

She says I'm pretty great as well!

She's like a mum, but unlike mine,

she seems to have just loads of time.

I go round to her house to play,

And sometimes we just chat all day.

She knows a lot more things than me,

But then she's lived for ages, see?

She loves the photos Mummy sends,

And shows them off to all her friends.

She takes me out for special treats,

And sometimes buys us bags of sweets!

We ride on trains, and buses too,

and have adventures. Yes, we do!

We play all sorts of brilliant games,

And give each other silly names.

We really love to cook and bake,

And eat the yummy things we make.

We watch my favourites on TV,

And snuggle up, just her and me.

She's got a very comfy tummy.

"That," she says, "is very funny!"

And when it's time to say goodbye,

My granny does a little sigh . . .

And says, although we've had such fun . . .

. . . it's nice to give me

back to Mum.

I hope your granny's just like mine.

We really have the bestest time!